Puppy Riddles

by Katy Hall and Lisa Eisenberg

pictures by Thor Wickstrom

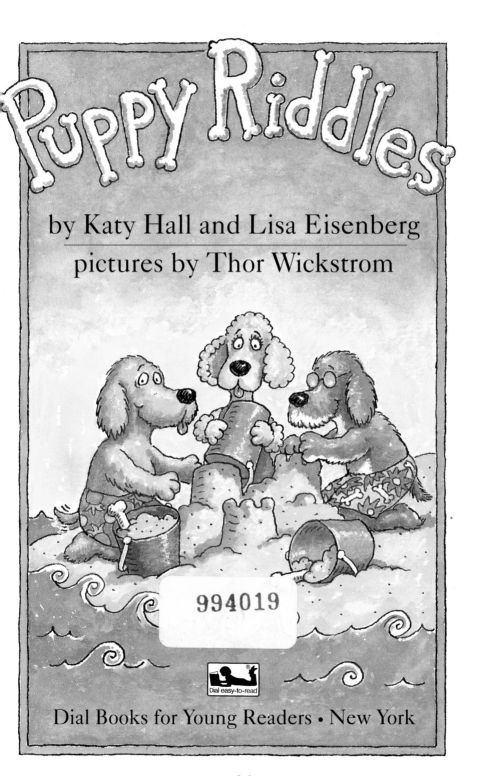

994019

Dial Books for Young Readers • New York

Published by Dial Books for Young Readers
A Division of Penguin Books USA Inc.
375 Hudson Street
New York, New York 10014

The Dial Easy-to-Read logo is a registered trademark
of Dial Books for Young Readers,
a division of Penguin Books USA Inc.
® TM 1,162,718.
First Edition
1 3 5 7 9 10 8 6 4 2

Library of Congress Cataloging in Publication Data
Hall, Katy.
Puppy riddles/by Katy Hall and Lisa Eisenberg;
pictures by Thor Wickstrom.
p. cm.
Summary: A collection of forty-two riddles about puppies.
ISBN 0-8037-2126-9 (trade).—ISBN 0-8037-2129-3 (lib.)
1. Riddles, Juvenile. 2. Puppies—Juvenile humor.
[1. Riddles. 2. Jokes. 3. Dogs—Wit and humor.]
I. Eisenberg, Lisa. II. Wickstrom, Thor, ill. III. Title.
PN6371.5.H34865 1998
818'.5402—dc21 97-6375 CIP AC

Reading Level 2.6

The full-color artwork was prepared using pen and ink,
colored pencils, watercolor, and gouache.

For Susie, Otto, Pixie, and Lucy
K.H.

For Tommy
L.E.

For Gertrude, Poochie, and Shark—
pups I have loved
T.W.

How do we know that puppies love their dads?

They always lick their paws!

Where do little dogs
sleep on camp-outs?

In pup tents.

Why did the puppy jump into the river?

He wanted to chase the catfish!

What did the puppy do
when she won first prize
at the dog show?

She took a bow-wow.

10

What did the puppy
say to the flea?

"Don't bug me!"

What would you get
if you crossed a mutt
and a poodle?

A muddle.

What happened to the puppy
who ate an onion?

His bark was *much* worse
than his bite.

Where do you take a sick puppy?

To the *dog*tor.

Where do puppies like
to go river rafting?

Collie-rado.

What song do little dogs
like to sing?

"Pup Goes the Weasel."

What do you call
a sunbathing puppy?

A hot dog!

What kind of soap should you use on your puppy's fur?

Sham-poodle.

What would you get
if you crossed a hunting dog
and a telephone?

A golden receiver.

What would you get
if you crossed an angry puppy
and a camera?

A snapshot.

Why did the puppy
feel so frisky?

She had a new *leash* on life!

What would you say
if your puppy ran away?

Doggone!

What do you call tough
little city pups?

New Yorkies!

Which puppy won the prize fight?

The boxer.

What kind of pups
did Count Dracula get?

Bloodhounds!

What is it when a puppy
dreams he's fighting
another puppy?

A bitemare!

Which puppies come
from Spain?

Cocker Spaniards!

Which baseball team
do puppies play for?

The New York Pets!

What's the main ingredient
in puppy biscuits?

Collie flour.

Which vegetables
do little dogs like best?

Pup-peas.

What kind of tree
do puppies like best?

Dogwood. They like its bark.

What's the difference
between a puppy and a flea?

A puppy can have fleas,
but a flea can't have puppies.

What would you get
if you crossed a puppy
and a kitten?

An animal that chased itself.

What do you call a fancy
American puppy?

Yankee Poodle Dandy.

Why did the little dogs
hold paws?

They were in puppy love.

What did the little dog
get for his birthday?

A new *collar*ing book.

What did the puppy say
when she stepped on
the sandpaper?

"Rough! Rough!"

What kind of stories
do puppies like best?

Furry tales.

Why are dalmatian puppies
so bad at playing
hide-and-seek?

Because they're always spotted!

How did pioneer puppies head west?

In waggin' trains.

Why do puppies run around
in circles?

It's too hard to run
around in squares!

What would you get
if you crossed a goldfish
and a puppy?

A guppy.

Why did the puppy go to jail?

He was caught barking in
a "No Barking" zone.

What does a mom dog say
when she wants her little ones
to quiet down?

"Hush, puppies!"

What did the puppy think
after he chased the stick a mile?

That it was far-fetched!

Which little sheepdog
can't find her sheep?

Little Bo Pup!

Where do husky puppies like to sleep?

On a sheet of ice
under a blanket of snow.

What should you do
if your puppy chews up
your riddle book?

Take the words
right out of his mouth!